Pippa Pennington

Sniffer

Illustrated by Eitatsu

Sniffer loved to sniff, and the things he loved most of all were the smelliest things he could find. His nose would go up in the air at the slightest whiff and he'd sniff.

He couldn't help going in search to find out what was causing such a smelly, smell.

"Sniffer, that nose of yours will get you in trouble one day," his mum told him.

Sniffer didn't listen. His mum didn't know anything about sniffing. He wanted to sniff all day long.

What trouble could it cause?

Sniffer opened his eyes one morning and saw the sun shining. Sunny days were always the best sniffing days. He stretched out his legs and gave a big yawn.

As he yawned his nose went up in the air and he smelled something. Sniff, sniff, sniff. Phew! What is that?

He looked around the garden. Now would be a good time to go and do some serious sniffing.

He checked around the garden once again, before digging a hole under the fence. He always got into lots of trouble for digging holes, but the smell was so good, he couldn't help himself. Naughty Sniffer!

Sniffer looked up and down the road and then trotted along, stopping now and again, when he sniffed something good.

He held his nose to the ground. Sniff, sniff, sniff, he went as he trotted along the path. Sniff, sniff, sniff.

Phew! What is that?

Sniffer put his nose up in the air.

Phew! What is that?

A stinky sock! Someone had left their sock in an open doorway. What smelly feet they must have. Phew! That must be the smelliest sock ever!

Sniffer ran over to the sock and sniffed. He pushed his nose right into the sock. Phew! Lovely!

Sniffer trotted on, until his nose went up in the air. Sniff, sniff, sniff.

Phew! What is that?

A dustbin! The smelliest, stinkiest rubbish bin he'd ever smelled. Phew! He had to get the lid off. He nudged the lid with his nose. Phew! It was so bad he sneezed. Aitchoo! Aitchoo! Aitchoo! Sniffer stood on the side of the bin until it fell over. Cor! All those smelly smells.

Sniffer pushed his nose into the bin. Phew! There were lots of smelly smells. Lovely.

As Sniffer dug his nose into the bin, all the rubbish came out all over the path. Sniffer sniffed and sniffed, while his tail wagged and wagged. Phew!

Sniffer was having a lovely day.

Sniffer had sniffed and sniffed the rubbish from the bin, but it made him sneeze. Aitchoo! Aitchoo! He'd better get away from the smelly bin. He carried on along the path. What else would he find? Suddenly his nose could smell something. Phew! What is that?

What is that smell?

That is disgusting! A big pile of mess that Growler, the big dog from next door had left. He should do his whoopsies on the edge of the road. Oh no! Was Growler somewhere near?

Sniffer looked around and put his nose in the air.

Sniff, sniff, sniff. Phew! What is that?

Was that Growler he could smell?

The smell was too good to be Growler. Was that something on the path he could see?

What is that? Phew! It smelled good.

Sniffer had to get closer. He crept along, keeping his nose to the ground. Oh, it smelled so good. He had to find out what it was.

Sniff, sniff, sniff.

As Sniffer got closer, the smell was bad. Phew! It was a big lump of smelly, blue cheese. Phew! Sniffer looked around. There was no sign of Growler. He ran up to the cheese and sniffed. Sniff, sniff, sniff. Lovely!

Oh no! Who can you see?

Sniffer took a bite. Yum, yum! Smelly, blue cheese tastes good. He took another bite and then another. Suddenly, Sniffer smelled something different. He looked up. Oh no! It was Growler!

Growler wanted the cheese. "Grrr! That's my cheese. I've been keeping my eye on that," he said.

Sniffer ran as fast as he could. Back past the whoopsy, back past the smelly sock, back past the rubbish bin, and all the way back into his garden.

Sniffer had never been so frightened.

Mum watched as Sniffer crawled under the fence. "Where have you been, Sniffer?"

Sniffer looked guilty. "Just sniffing."

Mum shook her head. "And sniffing got you into trouble, didn't it?" she said.

Sniffer looked sadly at the ground. "I just wanted to run home fast. I missed you." There was a big bang on the fence and Growler stuck his head through the hole.

"Looks like Growler missed you this time, Sniffer," Mum said.

Lucky for Sniffer, Growler was too big for the hole. Sniffer went to his kennel. He was safe. That was a lucky escape. He closed his eyes. All that sniffing was hard work. He didn't want to go sniffing ever again. Sniffer fell asleep. It was good to be home.

Suddenly, his eye popped open and his nose went up in the air. Phew! What is that?

Oh no! What do you think Sniffer is going to do next?

More picture books by Pippa Pennington:

Sniffer at the Beach

Sniffer's nose leads him to the beach where he finds himself in trouble with crabs, sandcastles, fishermen and seaweed. Then… Worst of all… The dog catcher. Run, Sniffer! Run!

Sniffer at the Farm

Sniffer manages to get chased by a turkey and tossed into the air by a ram when his nose takes him too close. These are only two of the animals he meets… Could his day get any worse?

Sniffer's First Christmas

Sniffer finds himself in trouble when he helps himself to the mince pies and turkey. He couldn't help himself… They smelled so good.

Join my mailing list for free e-books, news of new releases, and special offers.
http://book.adventureswithsniffer.com

Acknowledgements

I would like to thank Sid, Evie, Grace and Emily for their valuable help and reactions to Sniffer. You were an inspiration.